Sitting Bull Remembers

Sitting Bull Remembers

ANN TURNER

PAINTINGS BY
WENDELL MINOR

HARPERCOLLINSPUBLISHERS

*I*n this dark room,

in this place of fences, strange smells,

and men with yellow eyes

where finally I am caught

and cannot get free,

I close my eyes and am home again. . . .

The grass smells of sun,

rivers sparkle like the eyes of a child,

our tipis make circles on the earth,

and we want for nothing.

I see horses galloping:

dappled, gray, roan,

one like the fading sunset,

another like silver rain;

and each one carries a memory.

I was only fourteen when I first counted coup
by striking an enemy warrior's head
and earned my new name, "Sitting Bull."
It is a name of power and strength
that came to my father in a dream.
He gave me a shield painted with
sacred pictures to protect me.
I carried it always into battle.

My father and uncles taught me
how to be part of the Sioux Nation:
to be generous, open our tipis to strangers,
be kind to the young and old,
and fierce in battle, for we are a warrior people.
Once, chasing buffalo, an older man's
bow broke and he could not shoot.
Another hunter lost his horse early in the chase.
That day I shot four buffalo and gave away two,
so no one would go to his tipi empty-handed.

But when the Wasicu, the white people, came,
it all changed. They laid strips of hard metal
over our earth, deep in Sioux territory.
Though we fought hard, they built their railroad,
and noise and smoke and greed
came to stay in our land.
They thought you could own it and sell it,
piece by piece,
like a man lifting a handful of earth
to weigh on a white man's scale.
They killed the buffalo for sport or hides
and left them to rot on the ground.
I do not understand such ways.
They are not the way of the Sioux.

The soldiers marched deep
into Sioux territory. Long Hair,
the man called Custer,
led a party into the Black Hills,
for the army and to seek gold.
We called it the walk of thieves,
for that is *our* sacred land, the treaties agreed.

How could they break their word
for the sake of a yellow rock?
Then a company of soldiers attacked
a winter camp on the Powder River,
and our friends had to hobble through deep snow,
without warm clothes, without food,
seeking shelter with us.

Anger grew in me and in many other Sioux.

When the grass grew green

a great number of our people gathered together—

the Hunkpapa, Blackfeet, Sans Arc,

Miniconjou, Brulé, Lakota, Yanktonai,

and our allies, the Cheyenne—

in a great camp by the river of Little Bighorn.

Before, we only stabbed back

when the white man thrust at us.

This time we would fight and win,

for did not my vision tell me so,

where I saw blue soldiers ride upside down

into our village?

That is a sure sign of death.

The battle came suddenly:
Smoke and dust rose over our village.
I heard the shrill calls of the women
as we darted and shot and harried
Long Hair's men until they were dead.
Some say I killed Custer, but it is a lie;
he killed himself by attacking so many,
hoping to take us by surprise.
Our people took paper money from the soldiers
and gave it to our children, who made blankets
for their clay ponies and shawls for their dolls.
That is all it is good for.

Even while we celebrated our great victory,
that was the end of our way of life,
though I did not know it then.
The general we called Bear Coat
hunted and hounded us until
most went to live on the reservation.

But I led my band into the land of the Grandmother,
which the whites call Canada.
Four years we held out
until I knew we must surrender or die,
for the buffalo had gone
and my people were starving.

Here I am—the one they wanted—
the medicine man, the war leader,
caught like a bear in a trap
without claws (they took my weapons)
and with only some of my people left.
Now the white men give us food,
and the once proud warriors are like toothless old ones,
dependent on gifts.

*T*he dream horses—each one carrying a memory—
gallop by in my thoughts
as I stare into the dark before dawn.

I remember riding swiftly over the earth,
hunting buffalo, and feasting on warm meat.

Home was a circle of hides on the earth,
holding the laughter of children
and the wise counsel of our wives.

Today I dreamed I rode my gray horse home

to swing down and pull my children close,

to sit by the fire and talk of grass,

sky, the ways of animals,

and the great light that shines over all.

$\mathcal{B}$ut when I open my eyes
it is all gone,
and only my voice is left,
telling of how it used to be.

HISTORICAL NOTE

Some remembered him as six feet tall, others as well under six feet. Whatever his true height, Sitting Bull of the Hunkpapa band of the Sioux Nation impressed people with his commanding presence. Sitting Bull (whose name is properly translated from Lakota as "Someone Wise Sits Among Us") was a man of character and spirituality, a superb horseman and hunter, a man who loved women and children. He was chosen to be the war chief of the Sioux Nation as battles with whites increased in the 1800s.

Sitting Bull had a deep affinity with nature and claimed to hear words in a meadowlark's song. One protected him from a nearby grizzly, warning him as he lay under a tree. Sitting Bull was a "Wicasa Wakan," a holy man, who created his own sacred songs. He could stare at the sun without flinching and endure sharp barbs piercing his flesh during the great Sun Dance of the Sioux.

But more than anything, Sitting Bull is remembered as the Native American leader who most resisted the presence of Wasicu, the white soldiers in the Sioux's land. (A Lakota Sioux translation of "Wasicu," pronounced *wah-shee-choo*, would read "those who take the fat of the land.") He feared that the tribes of the Sioux Nation might become "corn and molasses Indians," dependent on whites and their handouts. Sitting Bull said he only wished to be left alone by the whites; then he would leave them alone.

In 1869 he was chosen to be war chief of several united Sioux bands. This was an unusual move, but Sitting Bull's uncle, Four Horns, knew their survival was at stake. Conflict with whites over territory made it impossible for the Sioux to live the way they had on the Northern Plains, following the buffalo and moving about a large area.

After gold was found in the Black Hills ("Paha Sapa"), sacred to the Sioux Nation and providing good hunting during harsh winters, military pressure increased on the Sioux tribes. The government wanted them to stop defending their land and people

and to settle on reservations so wagon trains and settlers could safely pass through Sioux territory.

When white soldiers attacked the Sioux and Cheyenne at the Powder River during the bitter cold, the tribes knew that the soldiers had come to hunt and kill them. Enraged, many Sioux tribes and the Cheyenne gathered at Little Bighorn to fight back.

General Custer, an Indian fighter commanding the 7th U.S. Cavalry, thought if he could catch the Sioux "napping," he could defeat them. So he attacked the huge gathering of Native American tribes with a small force of soldiers and was devastated in the conflict. When the Battle of Little Bighorn was over, the tribes had lost about 100 people, while the 7th Cavalry had lost almost half of its men. The U.S. government was enraged, determined to "whip" the Native Americans and force them onto reservations.

Hounded by soldiers, many Sioux surrendered that winter of 1876–77, tired of fighting. Sitting Bull and his small band of Hunkpapas, however, headed for Canada, refusing to give up. But in the end, they had to surrender and go live on the reservation Sitting Bull so hated. No longer recognized as chief of his people, without arms, and forced to live in a log cabin, Sitting Bull's way of life was over.

Fearing the unrest of Native Americans during the time of the new Ghost Dance religion, which promised a glorious return to their old way of life without whites, the commander of Fort Yates ordered Sitting Bull to be locked up. The arrest got out of hand, shooting started, and he was killed by reservation police in the winter of 1890.

The attempt to erase the Sioux Nation is a tragic story. But we can take from this history an appreciation of Sitting Bull—a leader with vision, courage, and deep spirituality, who sought to protect his people at all costs.

This book is dedicated to all Native American
tribes who have sought to survive—and in
particular, to the members of the Sioux Nation
and to Sitting Bull's descendants, carriers of a
rich and inspiring legacy.
–A.T.

In honor of Sitting Bull and his
everlasting belief in the Great Spirit.
–W.M.

With special thanks to Robert Utley and Nadema Agard for their expert advice and reading of this material.

AUTHOR'S NOTE
Although *Sitting Bull Remembers* is based on historical facts, it is a work of fiction. As such, this book is
intended to explore how Sitting Bull might have thought and felt about the events that shaped his life. For the
sake of poetic narrative, some events have been compressed. This book should not be read as a biography but
rather as an imaginative exploration of the side of history that the facts cannot always give us.

ARTIST'S NOTE
I have made every effort to be historically accurate; however, some artistic license has been taken to create the
strongest visual story. My use of pictographic symbols, especially those based on Sitting Bull's own, is
intended to aid in demonstrating his vision as a great leader. Thanks to the Smithsonian Institution for the
use of its collection of Sitting Bull's pictographic images as reference for the paintings in this book.

SOURCES
Connell, Evan S. *Son of the Morning Star: Custer and the Little Bighorn.* San Francisco: North Point Press, 1984.
Utley, Robert M. *The Lance and the Shield: The Life and Times of Sitting Bull.* New York: Ballantine Books, 1994.
Ward, Geoffrey C., with preface by Stephen Ives and Ken Burns. *The West: An Illustrated History.* Boston: Little, Brown & Co., 1996.

Sitting Bull Remembers
Text copyright © 2007 by Ann Turner Illustrations copyright © 2007 by Wendell Minor Manufactured in China. All rights reserved. No part of this book may be used or reproduced
in any manner whatsoever without written permission except in the case of brief quotations embodied in critical articles and reviews. For information address HarperCollins Children's
Books, a division of HarperCollins Publishers, 1350 Avenue of the Americas, New York, NY 10019. www.harpercollinschildrens.com
Library of Congress Cataloging-in-Publication Data
Turner, Ann Warren.
    Sitting Bull remembers / Ann Turner ; paintings by Wendell Minor. — 1st ed.
      p. cm.
    ISBN-10: 0-06-051399-3 (trade bdg.) — ISBN-13: 978-0-06-051399-3 (trade bdg.)
    ISBN-10: 0-06-051400-0 (lib. bdg.) — ISBN-13: 978-0-06-051400-6 (lib. bdg.)
    1. Sitting Bull, 1834?–1890—Juvenile literature. 2. Dakota Indians—Biography—Juvenile literature. 3. Dakota Indians—History—Juvenile literature. 4. Little Bighorn, Battle of
the, Mont., 1876—Juvenile literature. I. Minor, Wendell. II. Title.
E99.D1S624 2007   2006029870
978.004'975244092—dc22   CIP
[B]   AC
        Book design by Wendell Minor and Matt Adamec   Hand-lettering by Anton Kimball   1 2 3 4 5 6 7 8 9 10   ❖   First Edition